The Bedtime Rhyme

Written by
Walter Wangerin, Jr.

Illustrated by
Benrei Huang

PARACLETE PRESS
BREWSTER, MASSACHUSETTS

For the love of our first grandchild
Noah Martin
March 28, 1998
—W.W.

For Ray and Chi,
my son's favorite grandparents
—B.H.

The Bedtime Rhyme

2008 First Paraclete Press Edition

Text copyright © 1998, 2008 by Walter Wangerin, Jr.
Illustrations copyright © 1998, 2008 by Benrei Huang

ISBN 978-1-55725-467-2

Interior design by Elizabeth Boyce

The Library of Congress has catalogued the first edition as follows:
Library of Congress Cataloging-in-Publication Data

Wangerin, Walter.
The bedtime rhyme/written by Walter Wangerin, Jr.; illustrated by Benrei Huang.
p. cm.
Summary: A parent eases a child's nighttime concerns by promising a series of loving and heroic deeds and speaking of a kind, wise, loving God.
ISBN 0-8066-3701-3 (alk. paper)
1.   Sleep—Juvenile poetry. 2. Children's poetry, American.
[1. Bedtime—Poetry. 2. God—Poetry. 3. American poetry.]
I. Huang, Benrei, ill. II. Title.
PS3573.A477B44   1998   98-11250
811'.54—dc21   CIP
                                                      AC

Published by Paraclete Press
Brewster, Massachusetts
www.paracletepress.com

10 9 8 7 6 5 4 3 2 1

Printed in Singapore

Are you my strongest?
Are you my smartest?
Are you my baby true?

Are you my laughingest,
Loudest and lastingest
Friend? Oh, I love you.

I love your eyes
Like fireflies;
I love your ears
Like boutonnieres;
I love your back,
Your bones in a sack;
I love your cheeks
And all your teeths,
Your nose and toes and tongue and such—

But you say, "Stop! How much? How much?"

How much, my honeydew?
How much do I love you?

Lay down your head,
My gingerbread,
And listen: I'll tell you!

If robbers should come
Into your room
To take you far away,

I'd put on skates
And I would chase
Them back to yesterday.

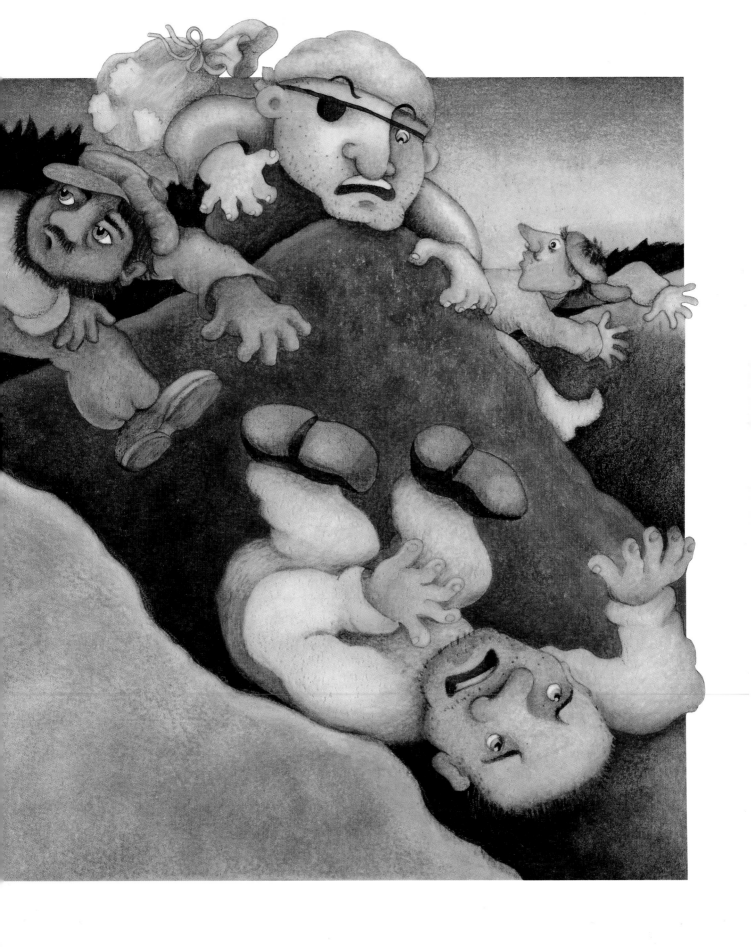

I'd clobber those robbers
Until they slobbered
And all their teeth decayed.

Then I'd bring you back
In a Cadillac
And hug you, my baby Grey!

Or if you should rise
Into the skies
On a dream of feathers and wings,

And if some star
Asked who you are,
Then scared you with fallings and things,

I'd follow you
In a gas balloon
And a basket that's hanging by strings.

I would tell that star
Just who you are:
A kid who is smarter than kings.

Then I'd carry you,
My baby Blue,
Home from your wanderings.

If monsters made shadows
Outside your windows
And rolled their eyes around,

And if they should mutter
And burble and bluster
And frown the most frightening frowns,

And if you were shivering
Under your coverings
Backwards and upside-down,

I'd grab my reaper,
My vacuum sweeper,
And suck those monsters down!

I would stuff them in stockings,
In bags and in boxings
And mail them out of town.

Then inside, outside,
Upside, downside,
On the roof and the walls and the ground,

I would write big signs
With underlines:
HANDS OFF MY BABY BROWN!

Or what if an owl,
The midnight fowl,
Should fly inside your room,

And land right there
On the back of that chair
In a raincoat, two boots, and a broom,

And stare at you,
And sing this tune:
To whom am I speaking? To whooooom?

Would you be bold,
My baby Gold?
Could you answer that bird: *To whooooom?*

And if you did,
Which name would you give
For the one with the owl in the room?

Your name? That's one.
But you're not alone—
If you call my name, I'll come.

So you and me,
That's two of we—
But there's three of us here! There's three!

Listen: before that hoot owl cries,
Before the monsters roll their eyes,
Before you fly above the skies,
Or robbers bother with alibis,
I'll sing you the bestest lullaby
  Of all!

Faster than I am
     And higher than stars,
Stronger than you are
     In both of your arms,
Here in your room
     All night while you're sleeping,
Kinder and wiser
     And best for safekeeping
       Is God.

That's the name,
My baby true!
That's the one.
Oh, God loves you.

From the brown of the ground to the blue of the sky,
From the golden dawn to the grey of goodbye,
From ear to ear a million years,
And butterflies both your eyes,
God loves you,
        God loves you,
                even better than I.

Now snuggle deep,
my baby sweet,
And here's the kiss to make you sleep.

Goodnight.